There's a Dragon in the Library

There's a Dragon in the Library

By Dianne de Las Casas

Illustrated by Marita Gentry

PELICAN PUBLISHING COMPANY

Gretna 2012

For Donna

In loving memory of Dannie Riley—Dianne de Las Casas

For Brayden, the best dragon tamer in the kingdom—Marita Gentry

Copyright © 2011
By Dianne de Las Casas

Illustrations copyright © 2011
By Marita Gentry
All rights reserved

First printing, January 2011
Second printing, November 2011

*The word "Pelican" and the depiction of a pelican are trademarks
of Pelican Publishing Company, Inc., and are registered in the
U.S. Patent and Trademark Office.*

Library of Congress Cataloging-in-Publication Data

De las Casas, Dianne.
  There's a dragon in the library / Dianne de Las Casas ; illustrated by Marita Gentry.
    p. cm.
  Summary: After seeing a green-speckled reptile hatch from an egg one day after storytime,
young Max tries to convince someone that there is a dragon in the library, growing ever larger
as it eats books, but no one believes him.
    ISBN 978-1-58980-844-7 (hardcover : alk. paper) [1. Dragons—Fiction. 2. Libraries—Fiction.
3. Books and reading—Fiction. 4. Belief and doubt—Fiction.] I. Gentry, Marita, ill. II. Title. III.
Title: There is a dragon in the library.
  PZ7.D33953The 2011
  [E]—dc22
                              2010029025

Printed in Singapore
Published by Pelican Publishing Company, Inc.
1000 Burmaster Street, Gretna, Louisiana 70053

There's a Dragon in the Library

Max loved story time at the library with Miss Donna, the children's librarian.

One day after story time, Max spotted a large, speckled egg on the bottom shelf of a book-case. He moved closer for a better look, when the egg began to shake and then—

Crack! Right in front of Max's eyes hatched a
small dragon!

Max ran out of the children's section to find his mom. "Mom!" he exclaimed. "There's a dragon in the library, speckled and green. He's a hungry thing! He's an eating machine!"

"Shhh," Max's mom whispered. "Max, you are so funny. Miss Donna must have had a really good story time."

"There really *is* a dragon in the library!"

Max's mom said, "Max, there's no dragon in the library, but you have a great imagination!" She laughed and patted him on the shoulder. "Come on, Max, let's go."

The next week, Max visited the library again. As he searched the shelves for a book, he spotted a wing on the other side.

Max followed the wing, and sure enough, he found the dragon. The dragon had grown and was eating a book!

The dragon opened his mouth and began to munch.
He filled his tummy with books. Crunch. Crunch. Crunch.

Max ran out of the children's section to find his dad.

"Dad!" Max exclaimed. "There's a dragon in the library, speckled and green. He's a hungry thing! He's an eating machine!"

"Shhh," Max's dad whispered. "You're right.
There *is* a dragon in the library."

"You believe me?" asked Max.

"Of course. Books are filled with dragons of
all kinds."

"There really *is* a dragon in the library!"

Max's dad said, "Max, there's no dragon in
the library, but you have a great imagination!"
He laughed and patted him on the shoulder.
"Come on, Max, let's go."

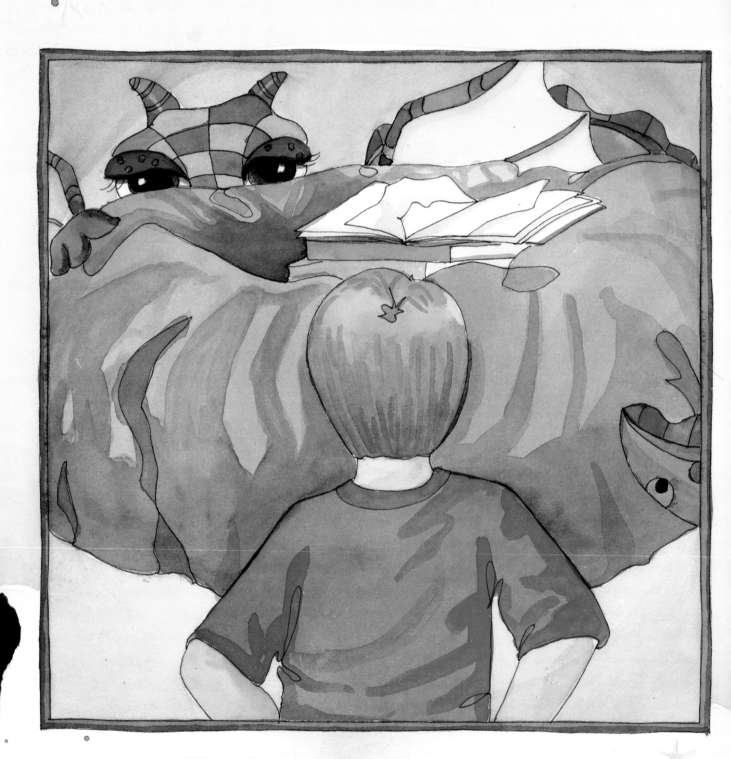

The following week, Max visited the library
again. Sure enough, he caught the dragon
hiding behind a beanbag in the children's
section.

The dragon, which had grown, nibbled on the book
Where the Wild Things Are.

The dragon opened his mouth and began to munch.
He filled his tummy with books. Crunch. Crunch. Crunch.

Max ran out of the children's section to find the head librarian. "Mr. Perk!" Max exclaimed. "There's a dragon in the library, speckled and green. He's a hungry thing! He's an eating machine!"

"Shhh," Mr. Perk whispered. "Really? Can you show me?"

"Of course I can!" said Max enthusiastically. He led Mr. Perk to the beanbags. There was no dragon, but there was evidence! *Where the Wild Things Are* was chewed at the corner. "See, Mr. Perk? The dragon was nibbling on that book."

Mr. Perk picked up the book and said, "I see. I think a baby, not a dragon, chewed on the corner of this book. It happens more often than I care to think about."

"There really *is* a dragon in the library!"

Mr. Perk said, "Max, there's no dragon in the library, but you have a great imagination!" He laughed and patted him on the shoulder. "Come on, Max, let's go."

The following week, Max visited the library with his class. He ran straight to the children's section to find the dragon. The dragon had grown to a monstrous size, and his head nearly touched the ceiling as he munched on a fairytale mobile.

Then he grabbed a book and began gobbling.

The dragon opened his mouth and began to munch.
He filled his tummy with books.
Crunch. Crunch. Crunch.

"You eat like a pig! You're going to eat everything in here!" exclaimed Max.

The dragon snorted at Max, and a puff of smoke rose.

Max ran out of the children's section to find his teacher.

"Mrs. Good!" Max exclaimed. "There's a dragon in the library, speckled and green. He's a hungry thing! He's an eating machine!"

"Shhh," Mrs. Good whispered. "How big is it?"

"Really big! He likes to eat books and other stuff. The other day he was eating *Where the Wild Things Are.*"

Mrs. Good said, "Isn't that one of your favorite books, Max?"

"Yes, but it's gone now."

Mrs. Good said matter-of-factly, "Your favorite book isn't at the library today because someone checked it out. It was not eaten by a dragon."

"There really *is* a dragon in the library!"

Mrs. Good said, "Max, there's no dragon in the library, but you have a great imagination!" She laughed and patted him on the shoulder. "Come on, Max, let's go."

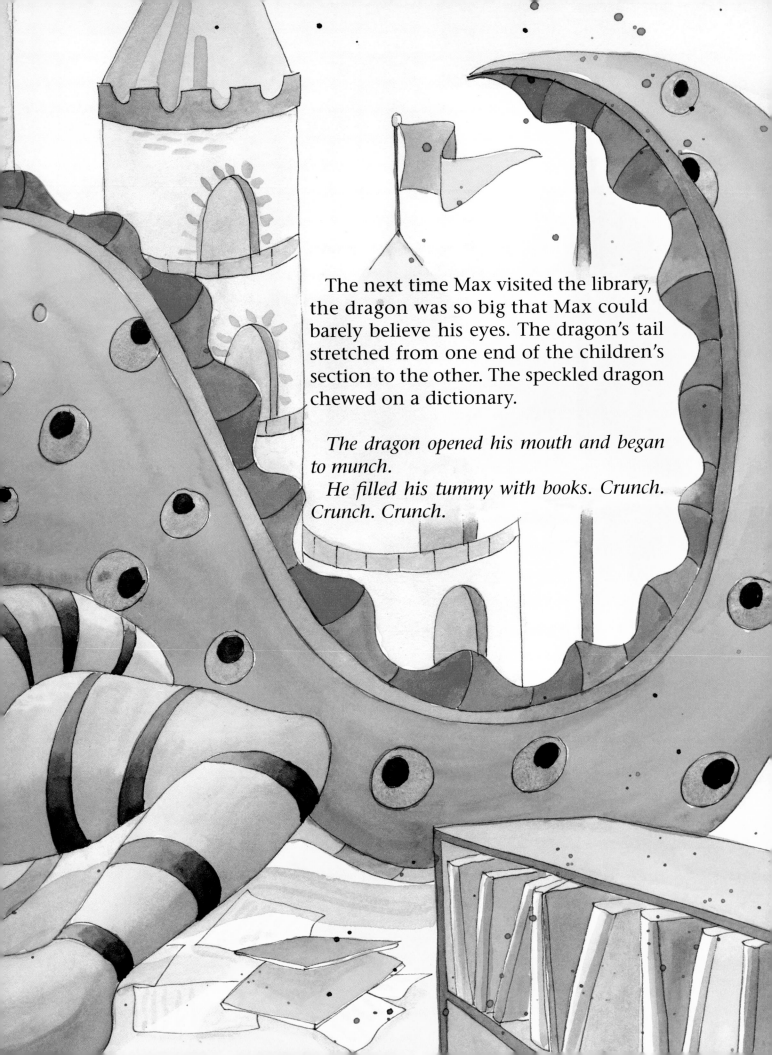

The next time Max visited the library, the dragon was so big that Max could barely believe his eyes. The dragon's tail stretched from one end of the children's section to the other. The speckled dragon chewed on a dictionary.

The dragon opened his mouth and began to munch.
He filled his tummy with books. Crunch. Crunch. Crunch.

Max scolded, "Books are for reading, not for eating!"

The dragon glanced disdainfully at Max and stuck out his tongue.

"That's it. I am going to tell someone who will believe me!"

Max ran out of the library and found Officer Riley.

"Officer Riley!" Max shouted. "There's a dragon in the library, speckled and green. He's a hungry thing! He's an eating machine!"

Officer Riley asked, "Is that so, Max?"

"Yes, and he's huge! Soon, he's going to eat up the whole library."

"Well, maybe we should check it out," said Officer Riley with an amused grin. "Why don't you take me to the library, Max?"

Max and Officer Riley marched to the library. They could barely believe their eyes! Standing outside, Max's mom and dad, Miss Donna, Mr. Perk, and Mrs. Good, along with the entire town, watched the spectacle in shock.

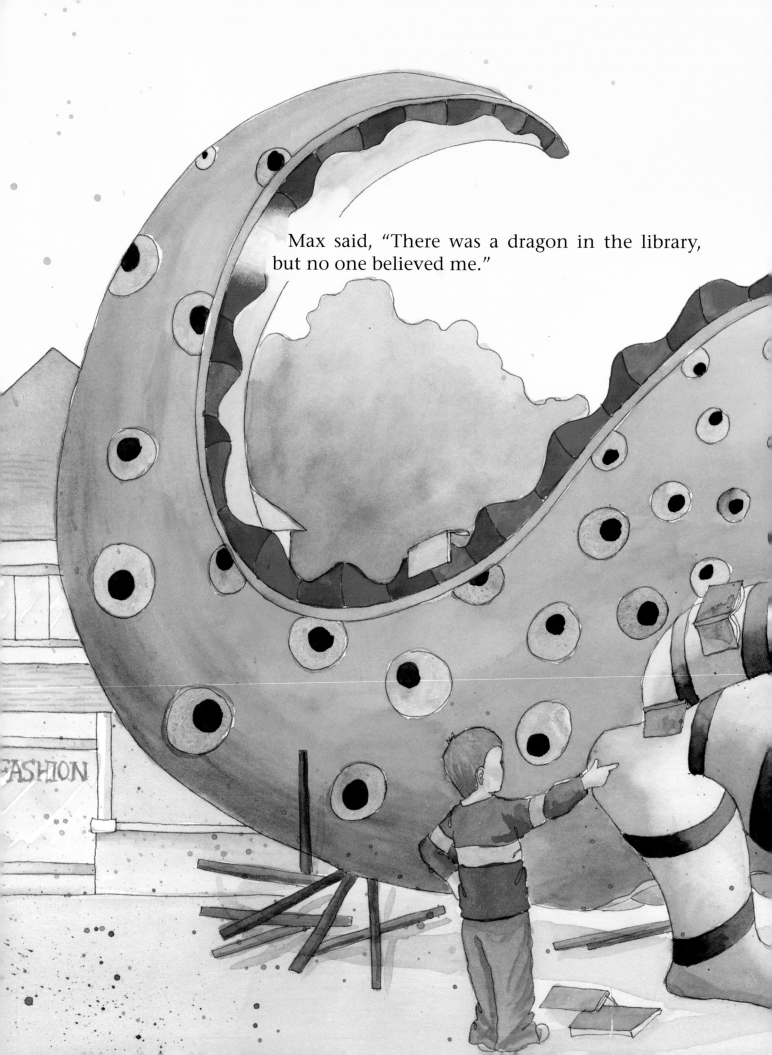

Max said, "There was a dragon in the library, but no one believed me."

"Now, there's a library in the dragon!"

Max's Book Care Tips

- Don't read in the rain, the bath, or the shower.
- Use a bookmark instead of folding a page to mark your place.
- Books do not make good lunch trays.
- When you take a book off the shelf, let a librarian reshelve it.
- Return your library books on time. Librarians *really* appreciate it.
- Never leave a book unsupervised near a hungry dragon.
- Books are for reading, not for eating!